MARVEL

GUARDIANS OF THE GALAXY VOL. 2

THE BEST STICKER BOOK IN THE GALAXY

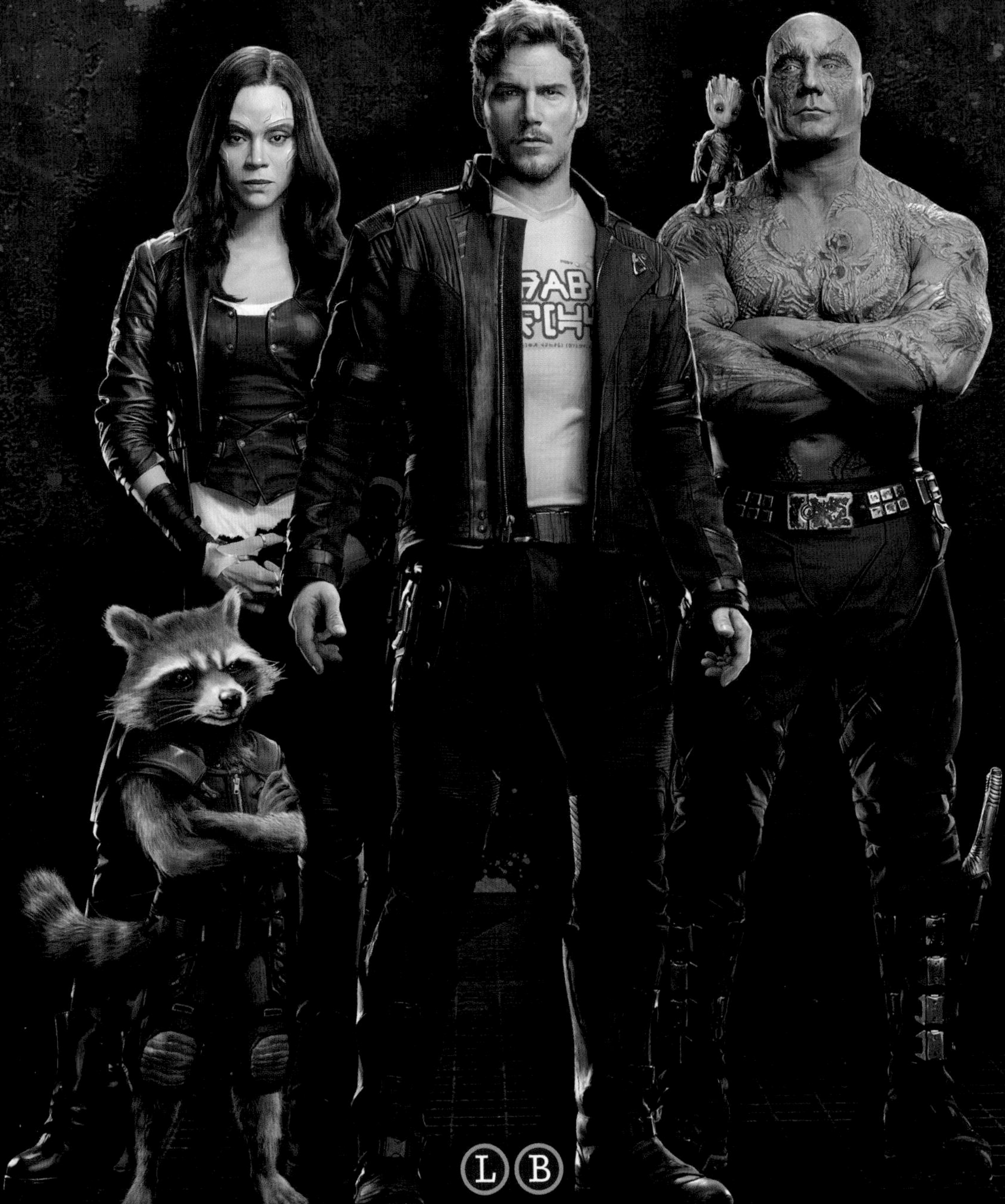

LB

LITTLE, BROWN AND COMPANY
New York Boston

Peter Quill, aka Star-Lord, hasn't been on Terra, aka Earth, since the 80s. Use your stickers to decorate his cassette like a real 80s kid would!

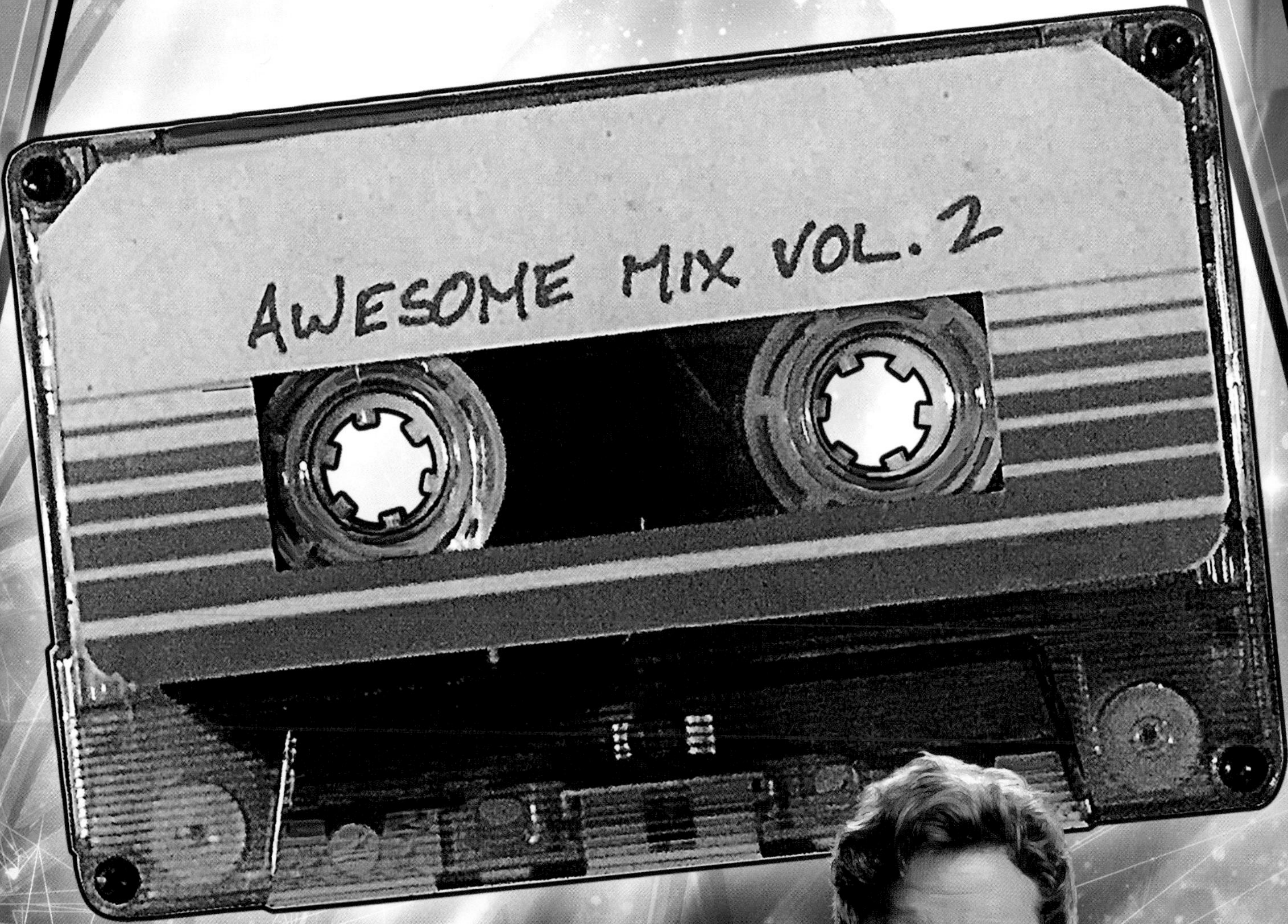
AWESOME MIX VOL. 2

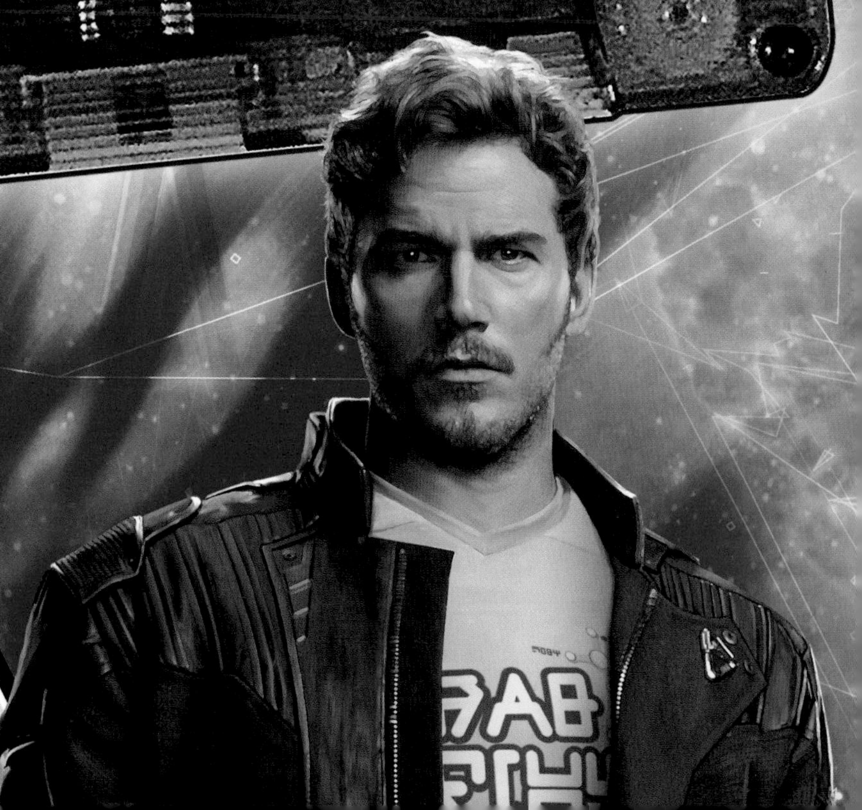

"I Am Groot!"

What Groot means is, use the stickers to come up with a fun new hairdo for him! He's sick of his growing bark.

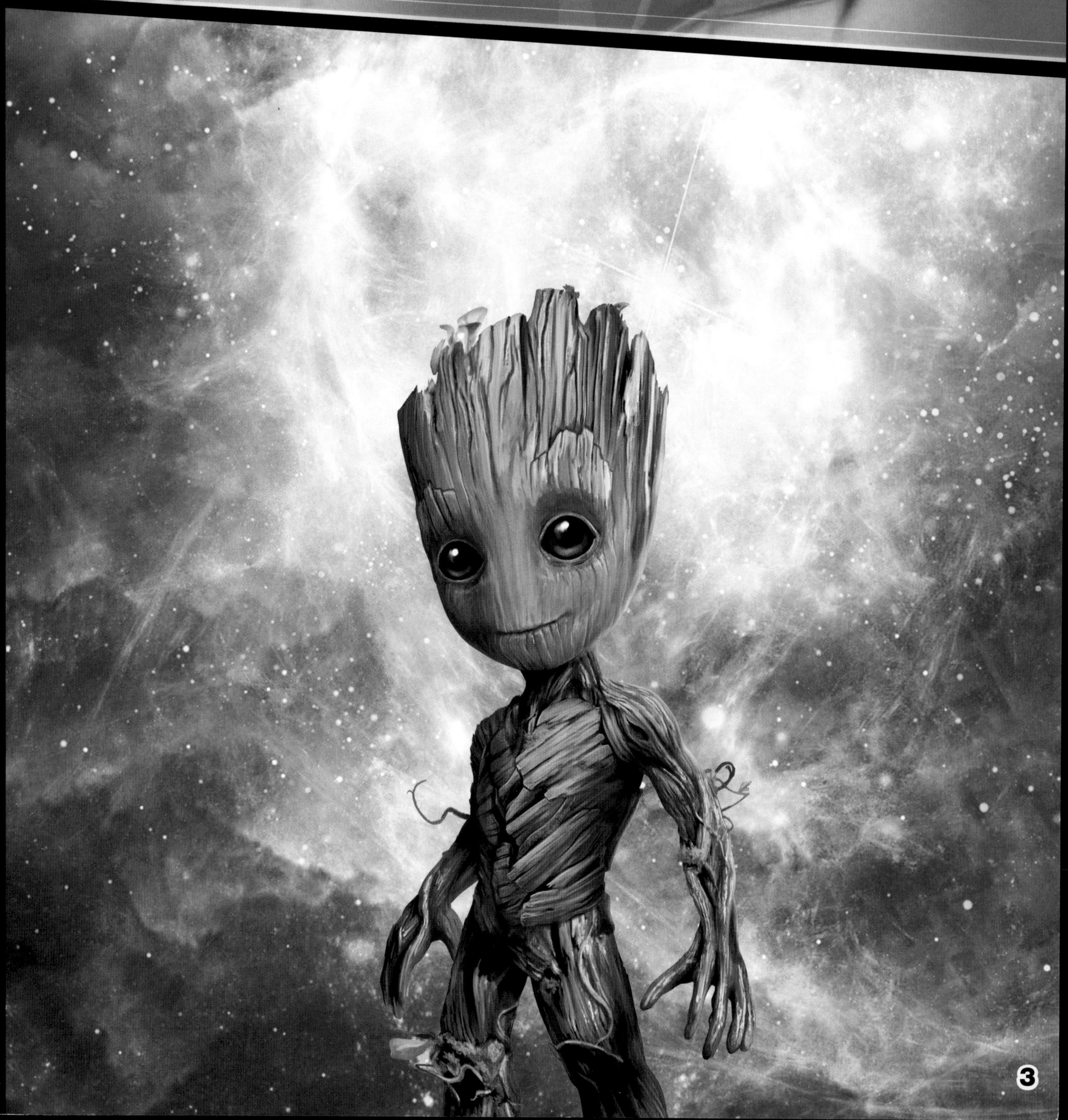

A Cool New Team Logo

The Ravagers have a symbol they all put on their clothes so people know how fearsome they are. The Guardians probably need a new one, too. Use your stickers to come up with some ideas for their new uniform badges!

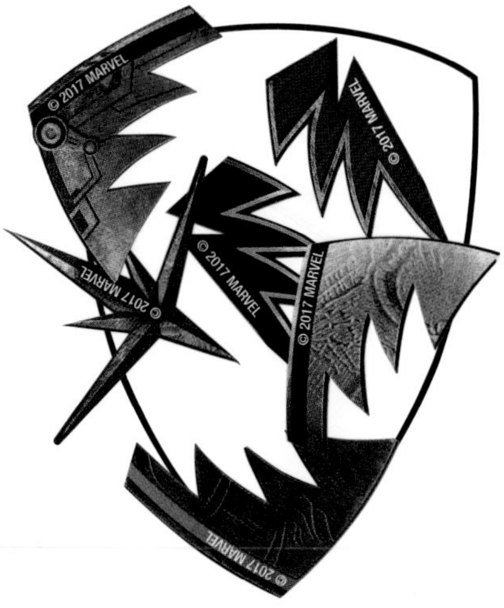
© 2017 MARVEL
© 2017 MARVEL
© 2017 MARVEL
© 2017 MARVEL
© 2017 MARVEL
© 2017 MARVEL

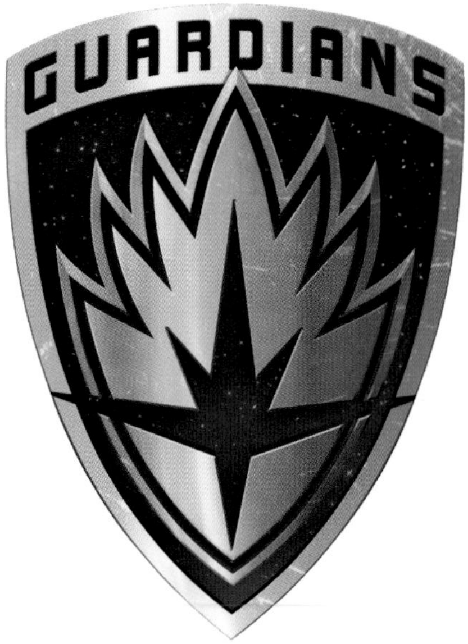
GUARDIANS

Now We're All Standing in a Circle! Great.

The Guardians of the Galaxy are still getting used to working as a team. Use your stickers to complete the puzzle below, and show the galaxy what it's in for.

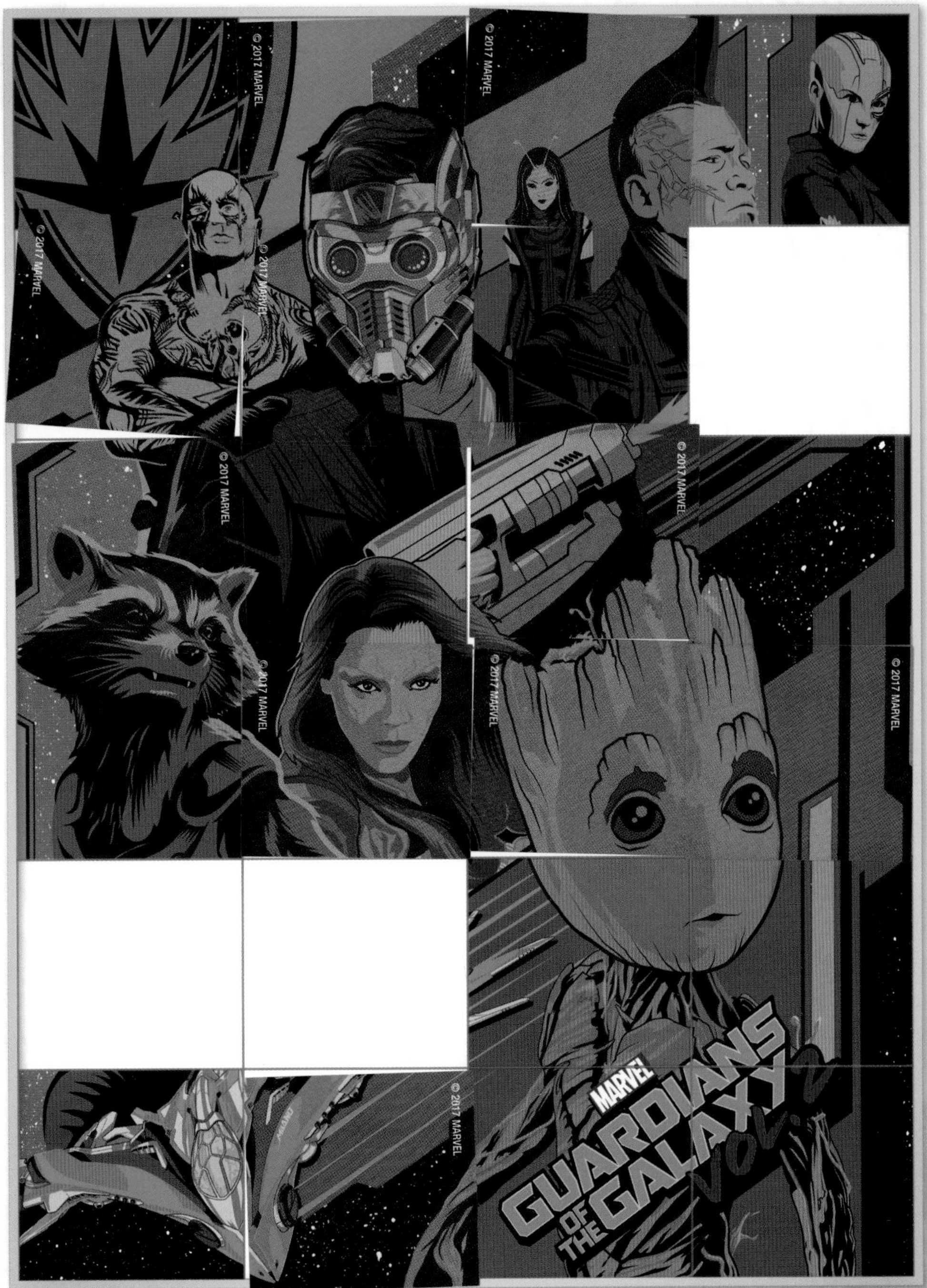
© 2017 MARVEL
MARVEL
GUARDIANS OF THE GALAXY VOL. 2

Names and Faces

The galaxy is full of crazy characters. Use the stickers to match the description with the right head shape.

© 2017 MARVEL

A "legendary outlaw" who leads the Guardians of the Galaxy.

© 2017 MARVEL

A mysterious newcomer, she is telepathic and an expert in martial arts.

© 2017 MARVEL

A living weapon, she is learning to show her softer side—occasionally.

© 2017 MARVEL

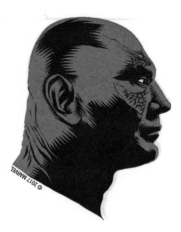

A huge warrior with zero concept of metaphor.

© 2017 MARVEL

© 2017 MARVEL

The leader of the Ravagers.

Gamora's sister and rival, she has a *lot* of robotics grafted to her.

© 2017 MARVEL

© 2017 MARVEL

Never call him a rodent.

Formerly the tallest member of the team, he says only three words.

Wait...How'd That Go Again?

Rocket is trying to impress some strangers by telling them all about the Guardians' latest big scrap, but he's a little fuzzy on the details. Use your stickers to re-create the top scene in the bottom box so he can remember exactly how it went down.

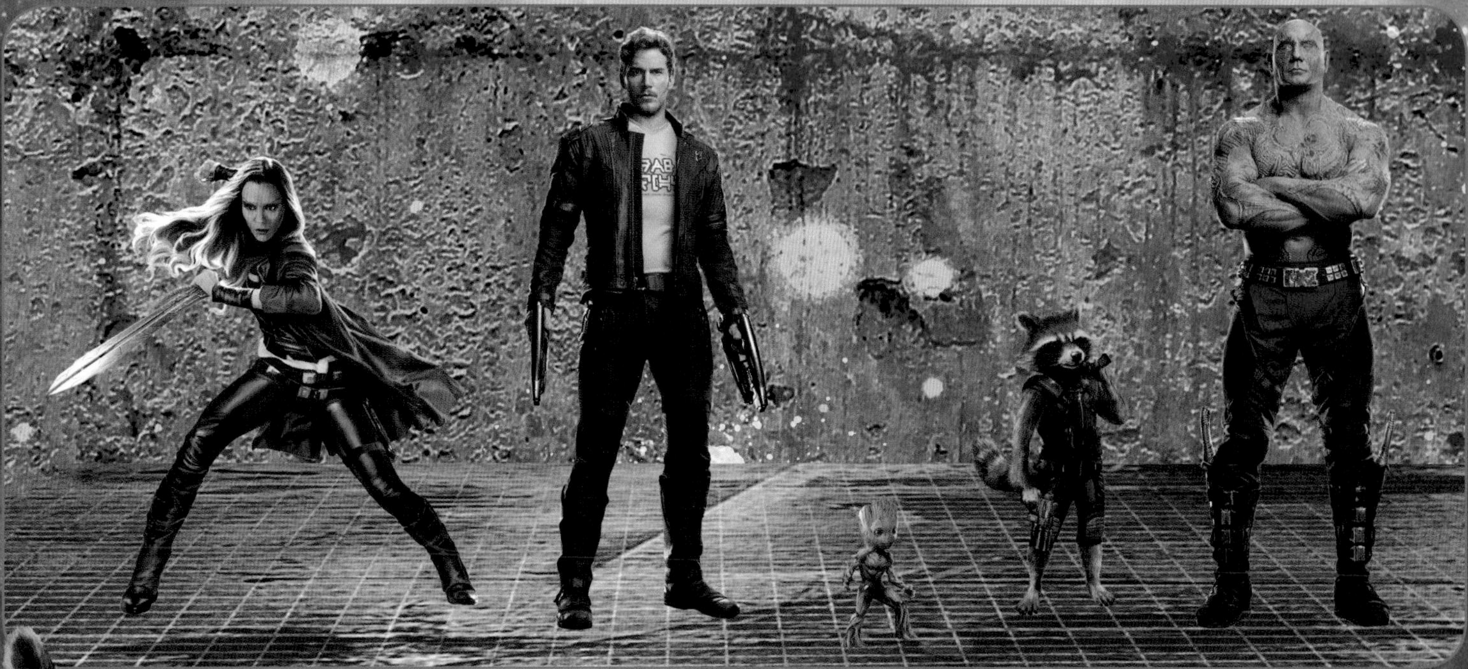

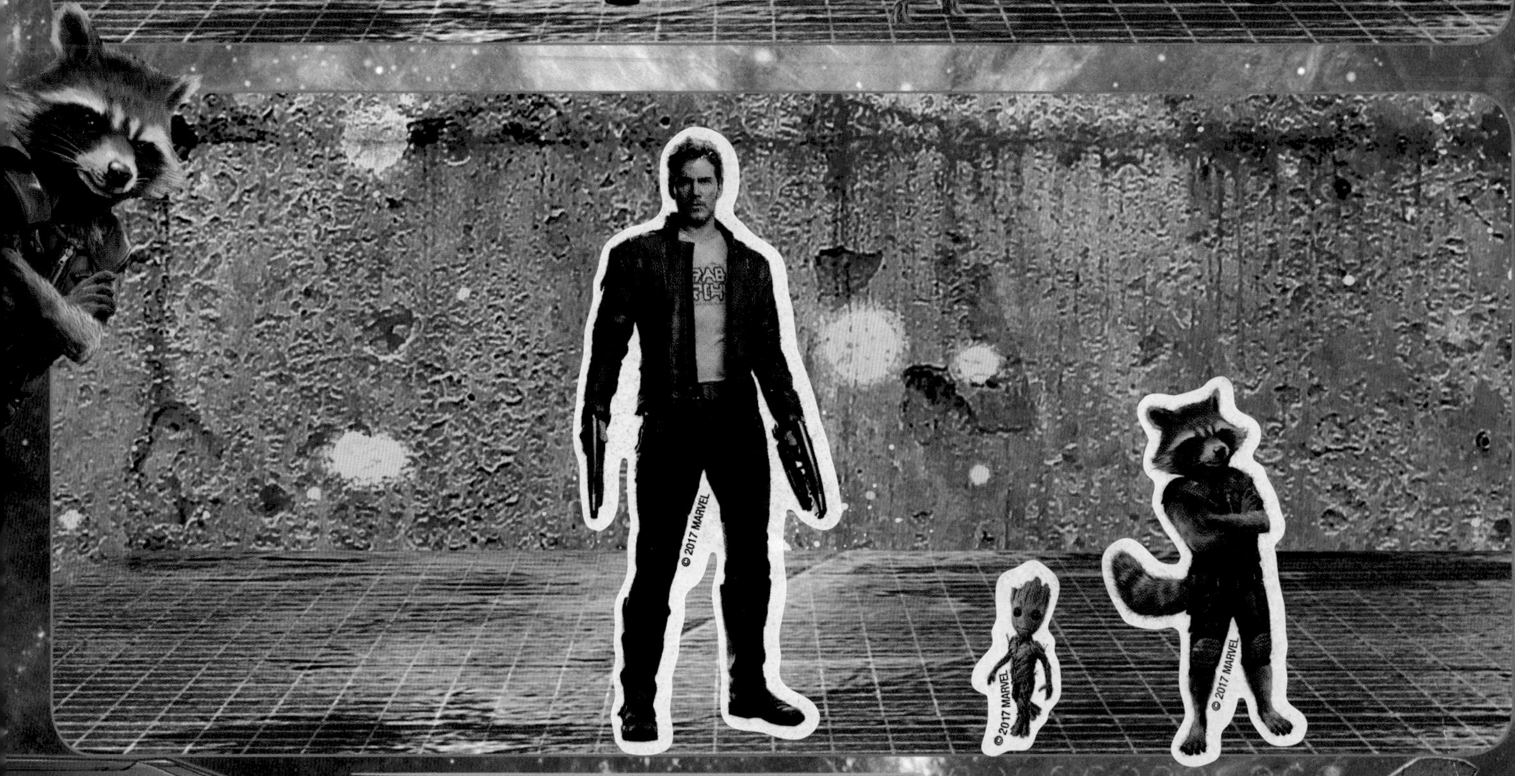
© 2017 MARVEL
© 2017 MARVEL
© 2017 MARVEL

Masks: Stylish, Practical, and Not for Everyone

Match the stickers with the numbers below to activate Star-Lord's awesome mask. The red eyes aren't that weird, right?

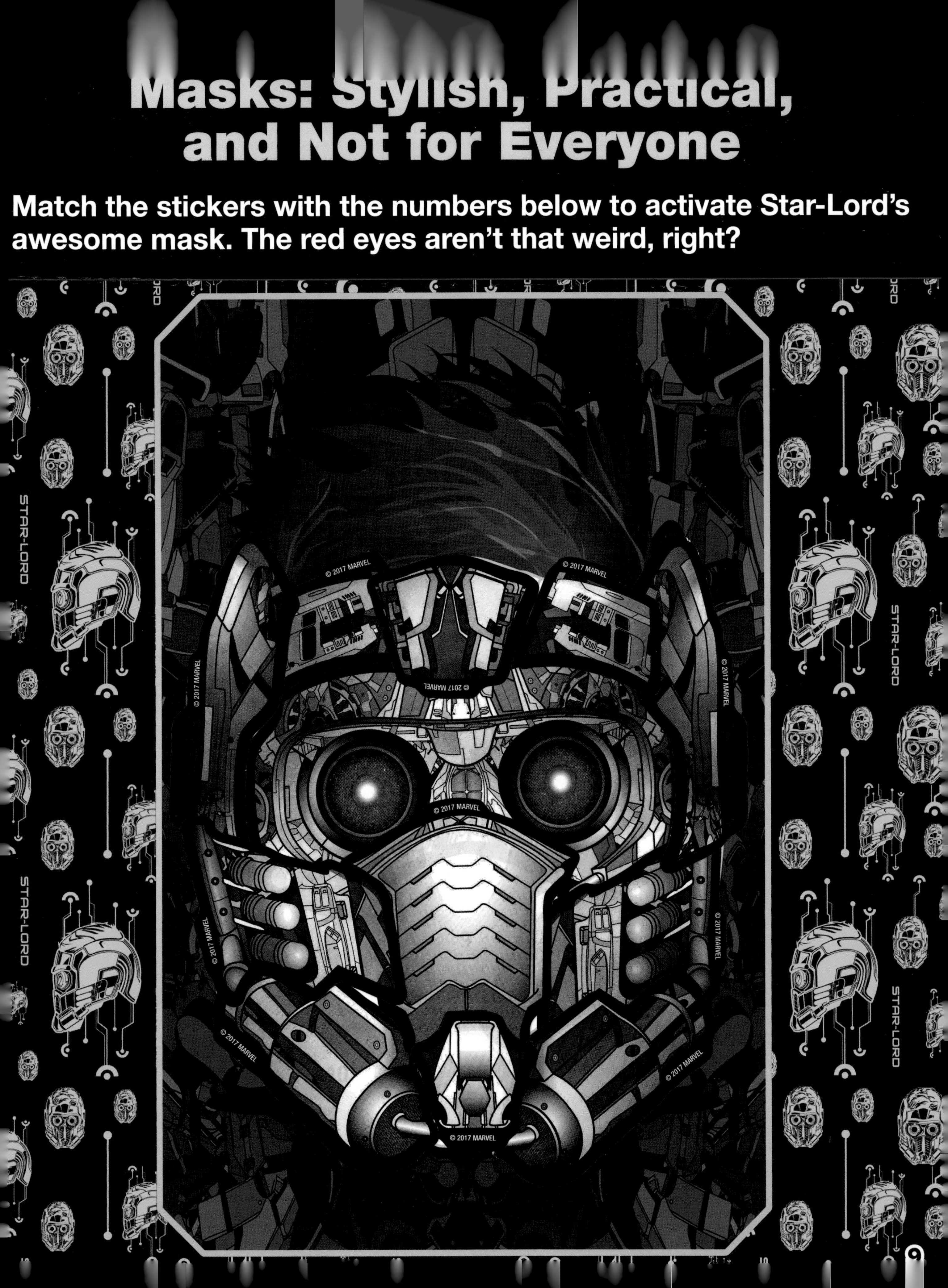
© 2017 MARVEL
© 2017 MARVEL
© 2017 MARVEL
© 2017 MARVEL
© 2017 MARVEL
© 2017 MARVEL
© 2017 MARVEL
© 2017 MARVEL
© 2017 MARVEL
© 2017 MARVEL

The Galaxy Is a Dangerous Place.

Space sure is big. Still…the Guardians can't help but run into trouble wherever they go. Use your stickers to create their most recent showdown!

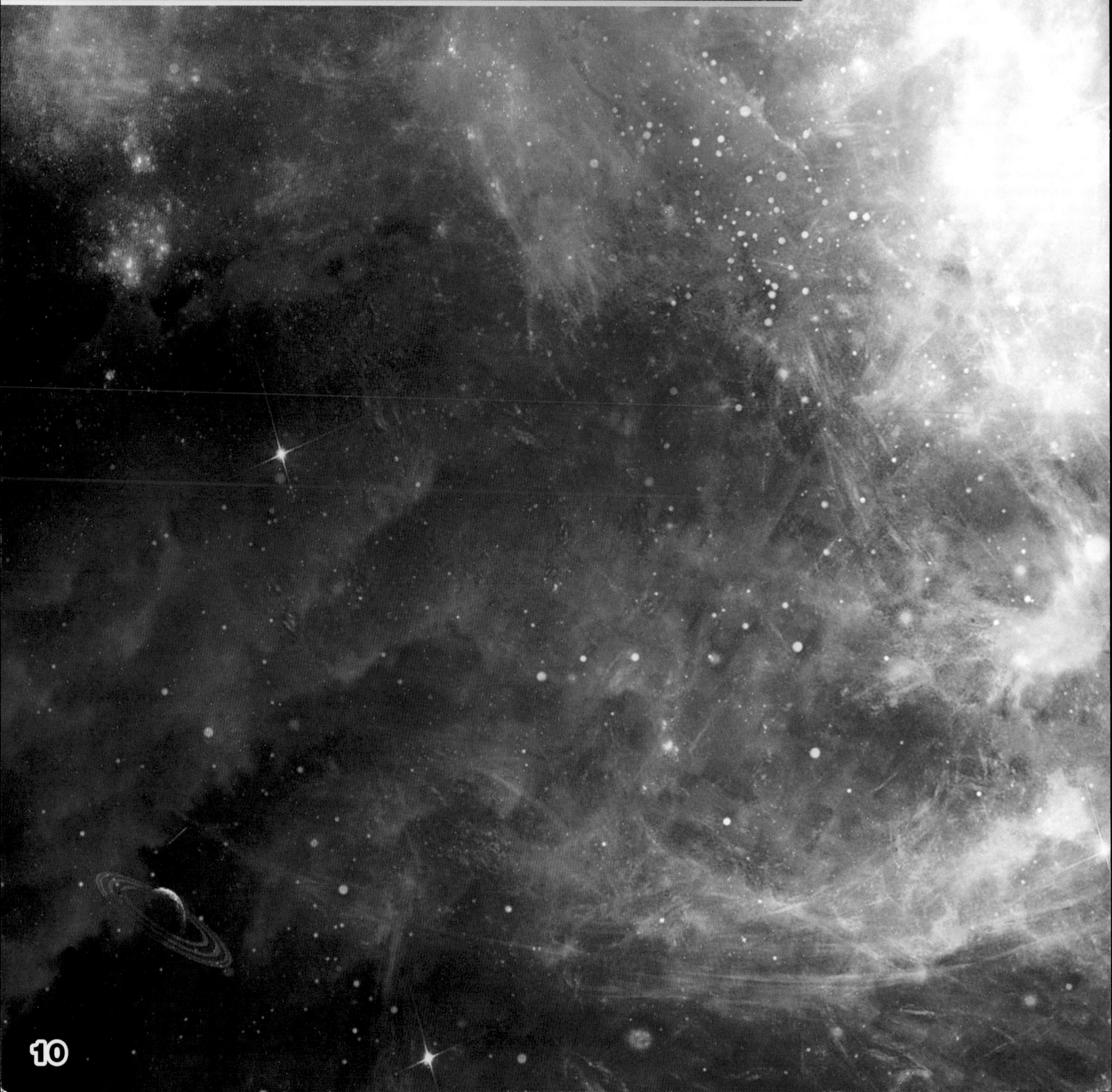

Some Friendly Competition

When Rocket and Groot have some time off after a mission, they like to play tic-tac-toe. It keeps them on *their* toes. Use their faces to play with a friend!

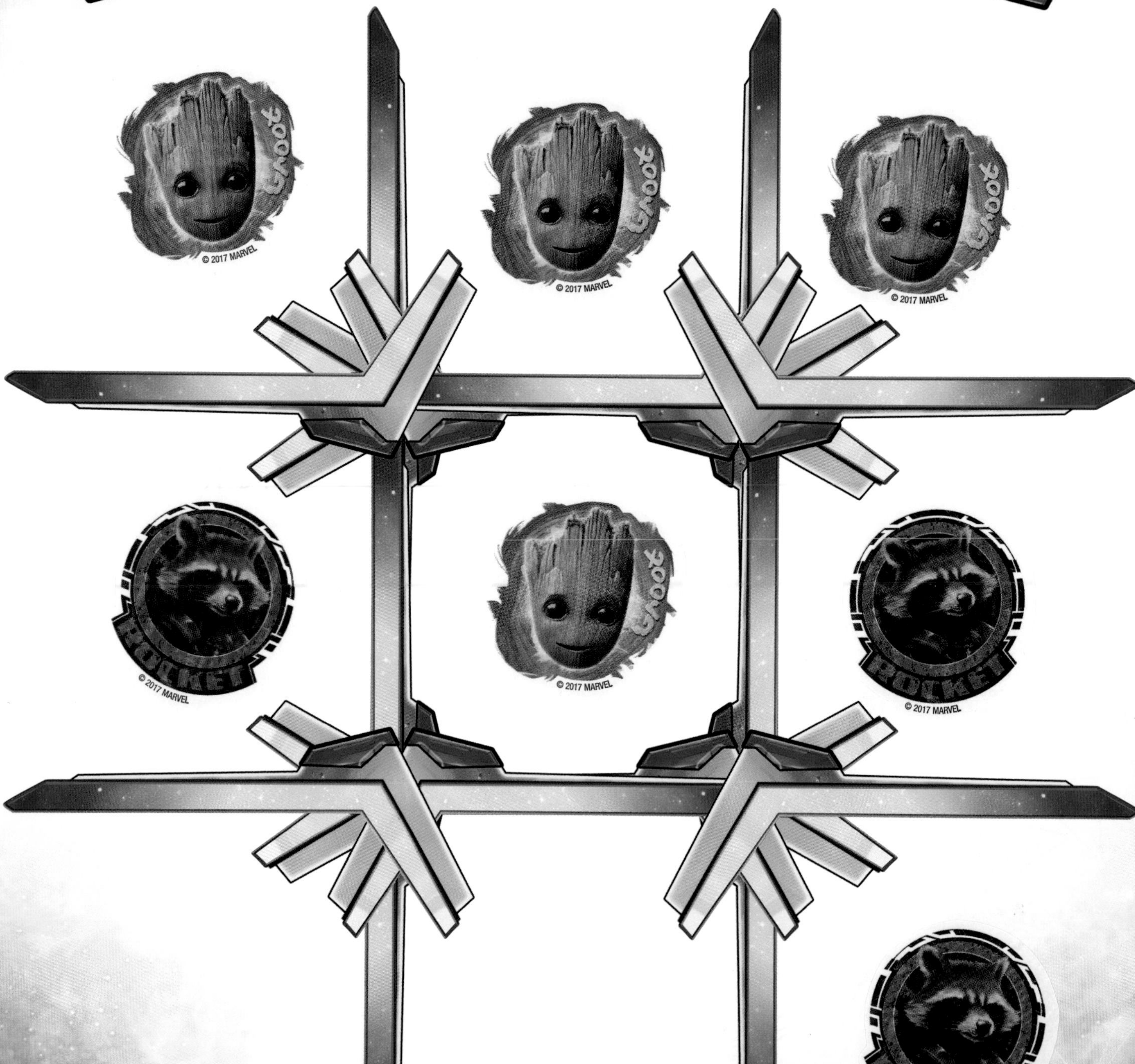

Groot
© 2017 MARVEL
Groot
© 2017 MARVEL
Groot
© 2017 MARVEL
ROCKET
© 2017 MARVEL
Groot
© 2017 MARVEL
ROCKET
© 2017 MARVEL
ROCKET
© 2017 MARVEL

PAGE 2

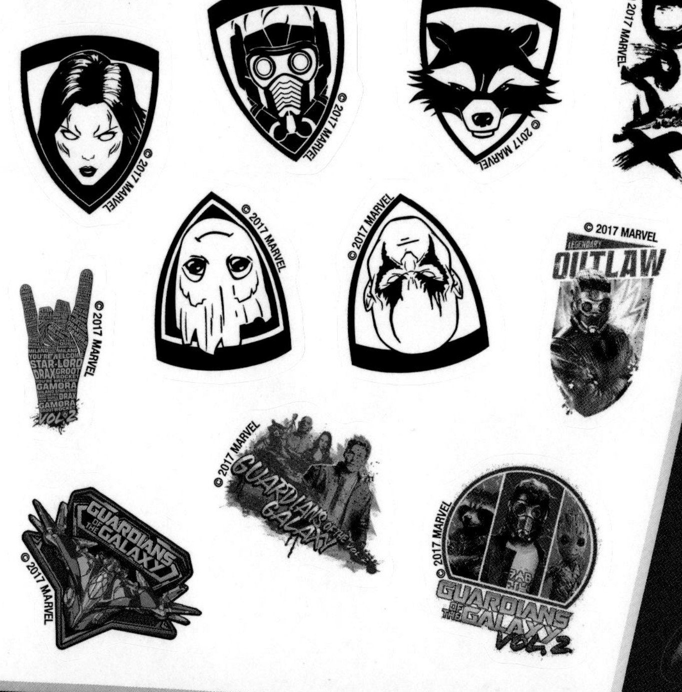
© 2017 MARVEL
DRAX
OUTLAW
STAR-LORD
GAMORA
GUARDIANS OF THE GALAXY
GUARDIANS OF THE GALAXY Vol. 2

PAGE 3

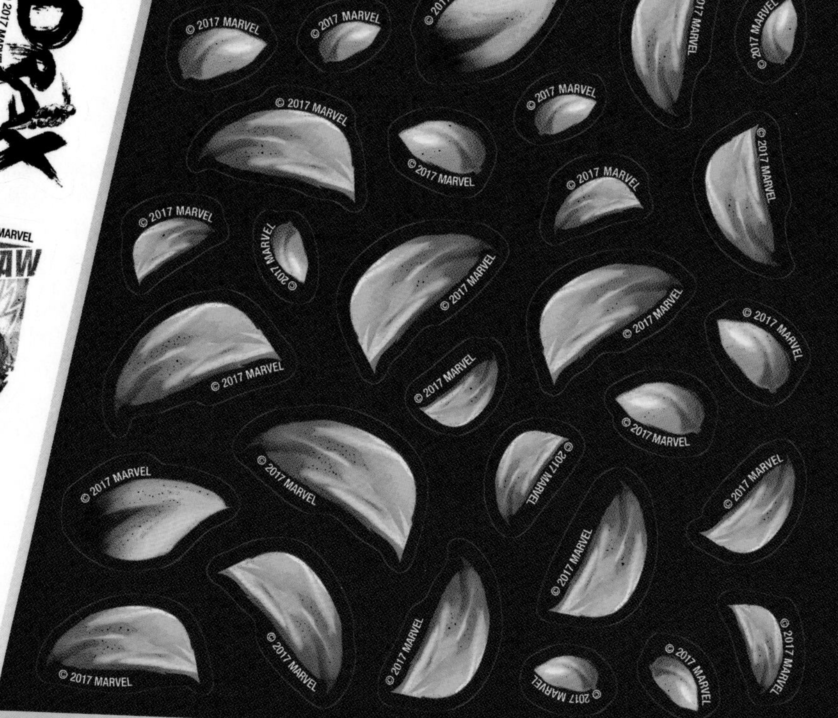
© 2017 MARVEL

PAGE 4

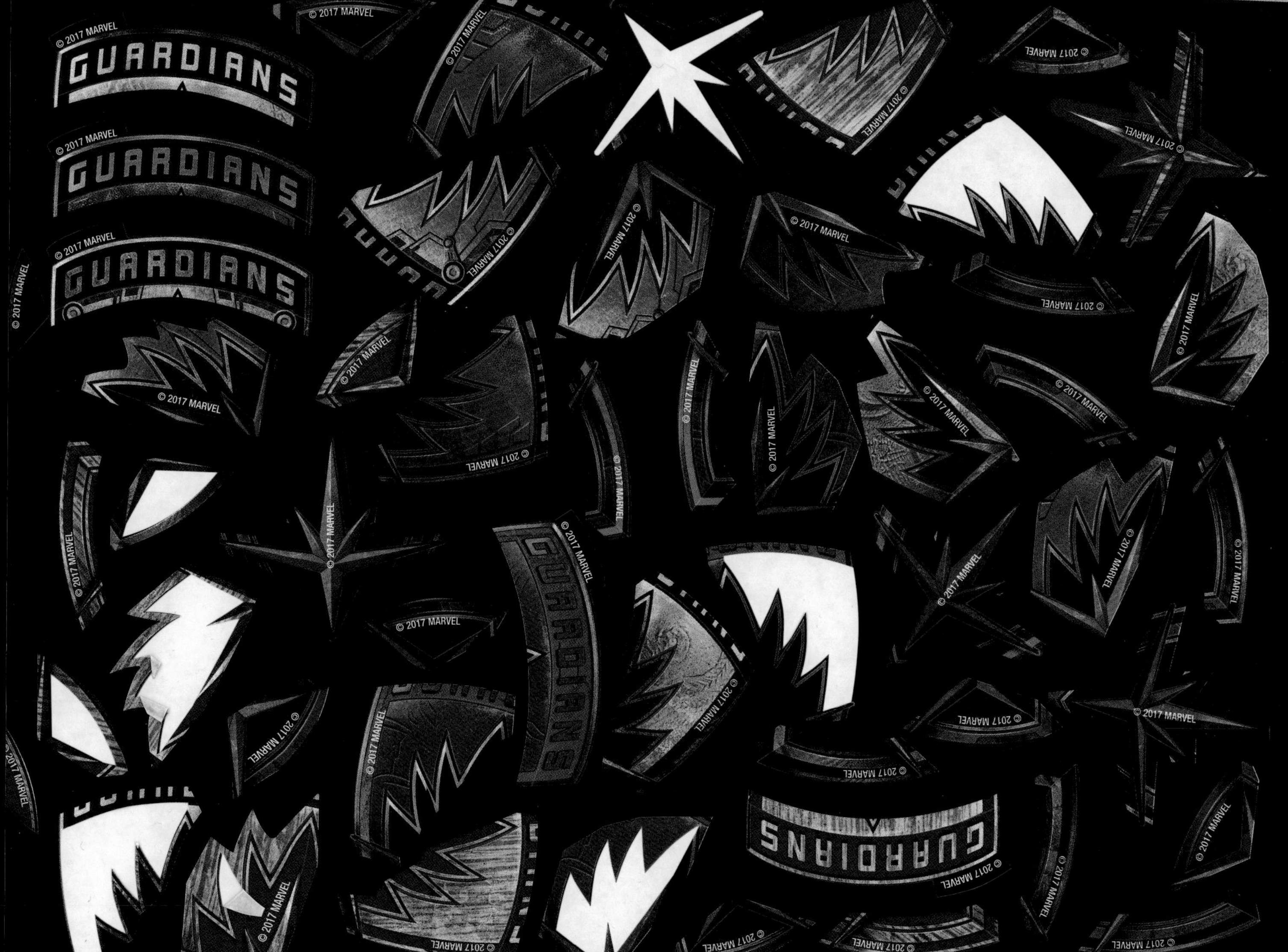
GUARDIANS
© 2017 MARVEL

PAGE 5

© 2017 MARVEL
© 2017 MARVEL
© 2017 MARVEL

PAGES 6-7

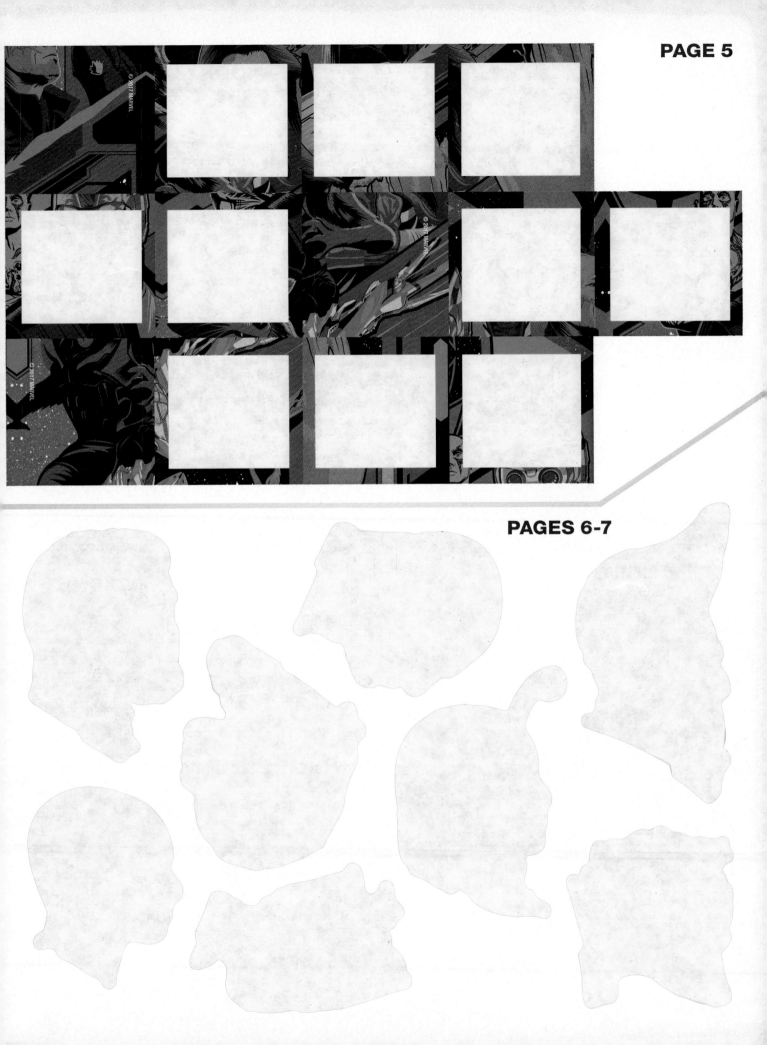

PAGE 8

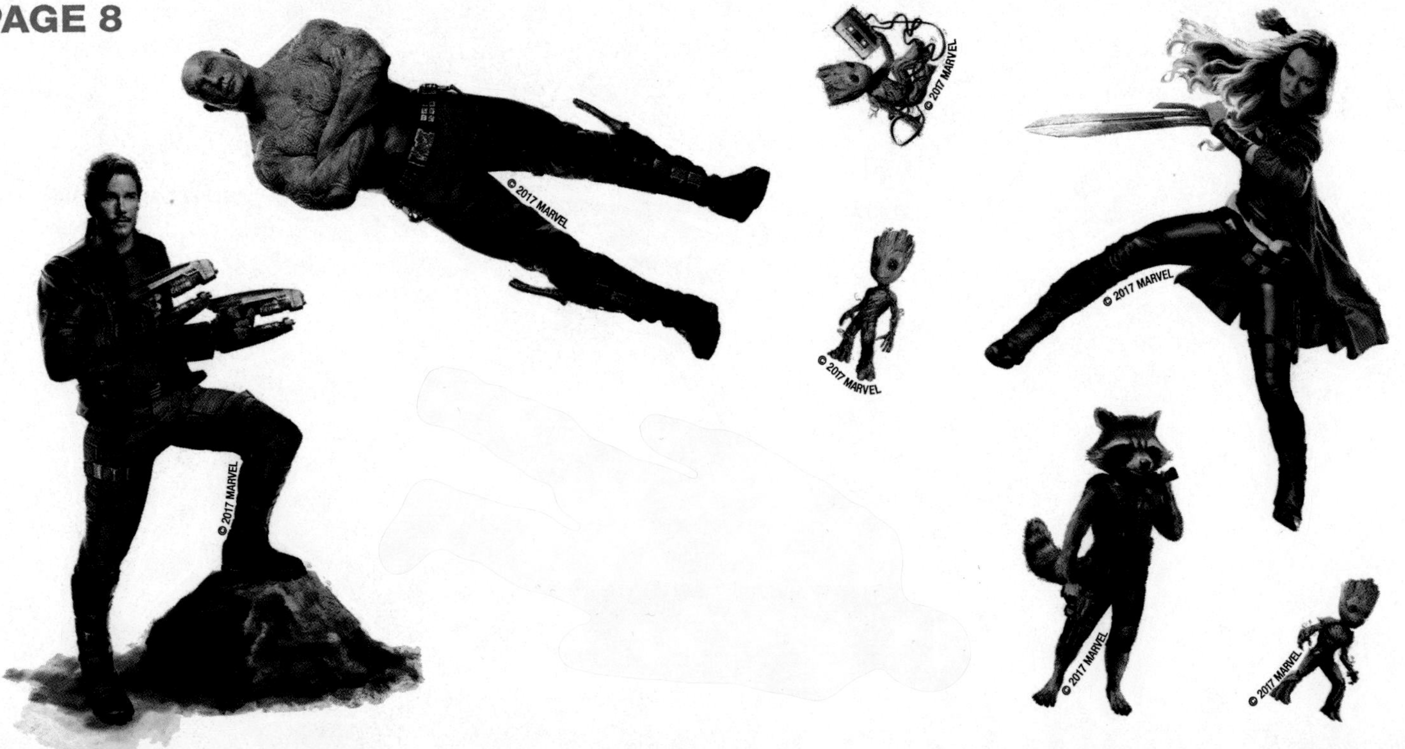
© 2017 MARVEL
© 2017 MARVEL
© 2017 MARVEL
© 2017 MARVEL
© 2017 MARVEL
© 2017 MARVEL
© 2017 MARVEL

PAGE 9

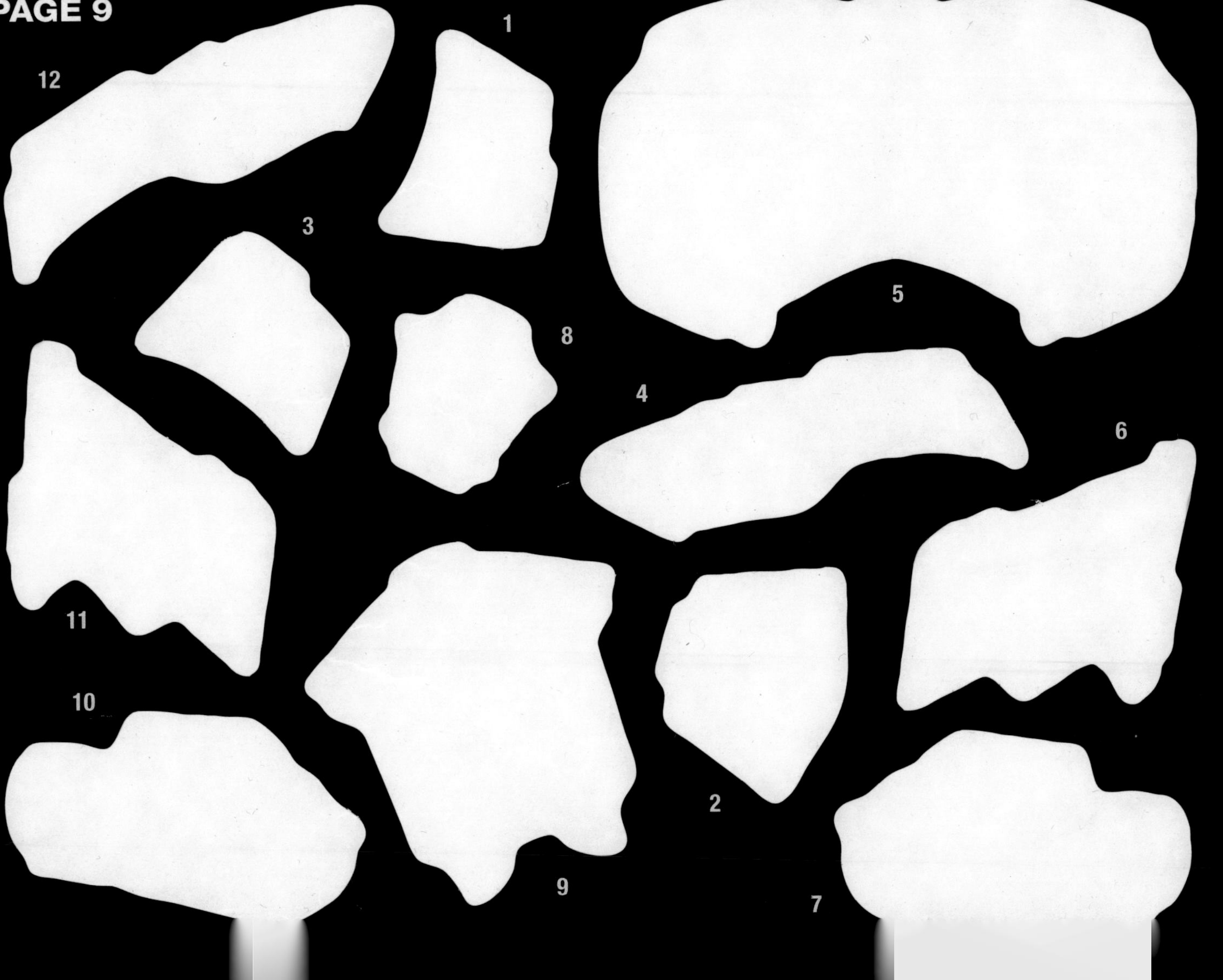
1
12
3
5
8
4
6
11
10
2
9
7

PAGES 10-11

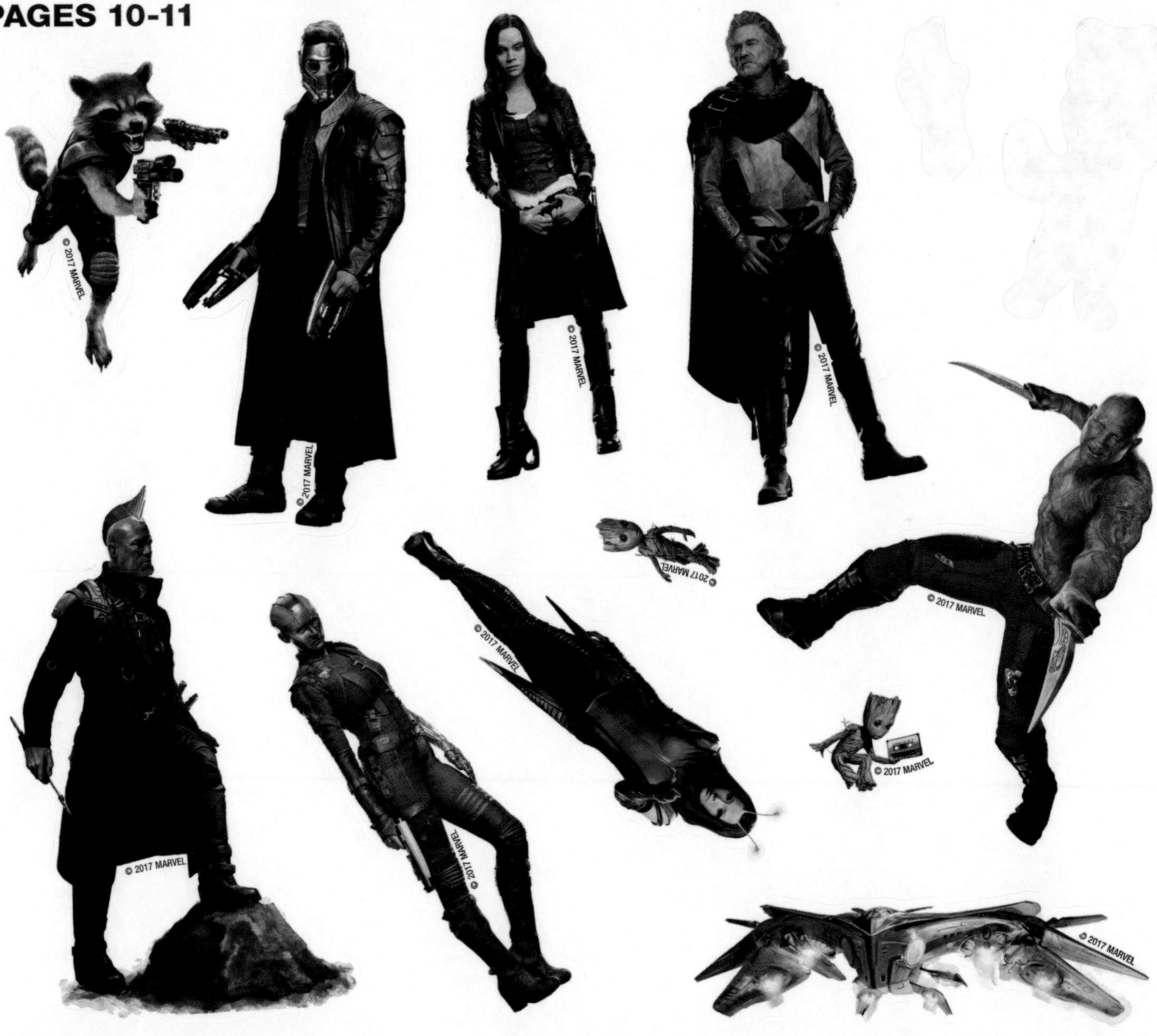
© 2017 MARVEL

PAGE 12

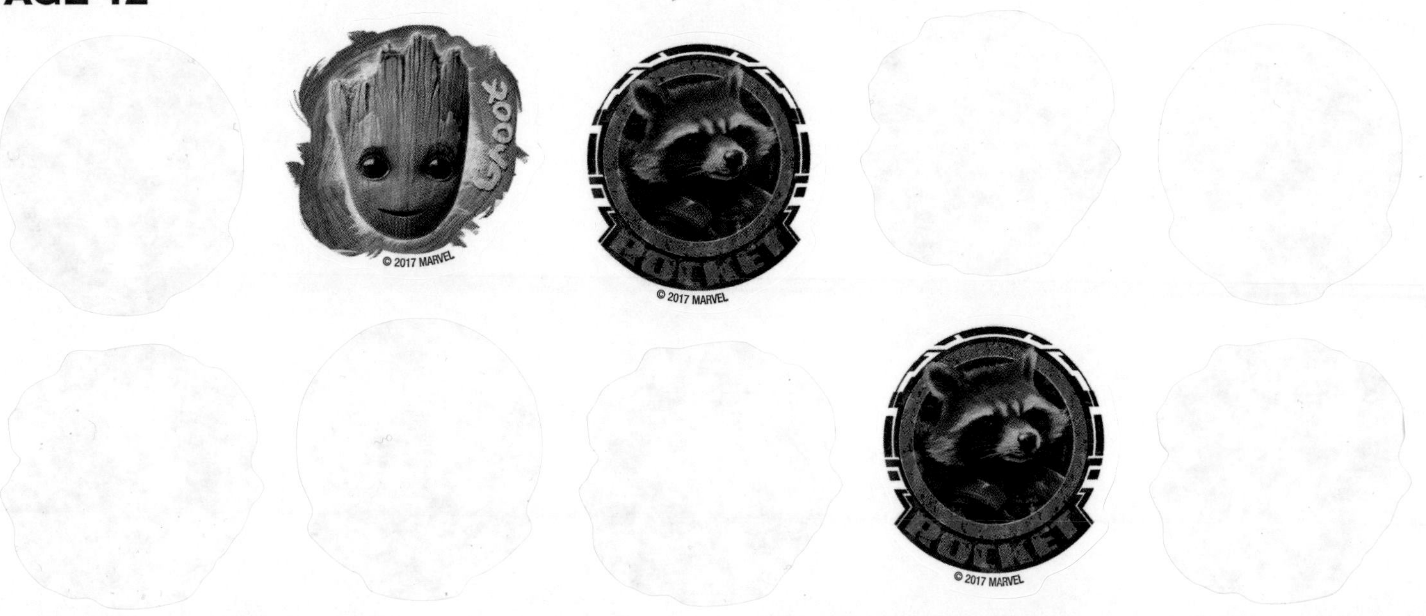
Groot
© 2017 MARVEL
ROCKET
© 2017 MARVEL
ROCKET
© 2017 MARVEL